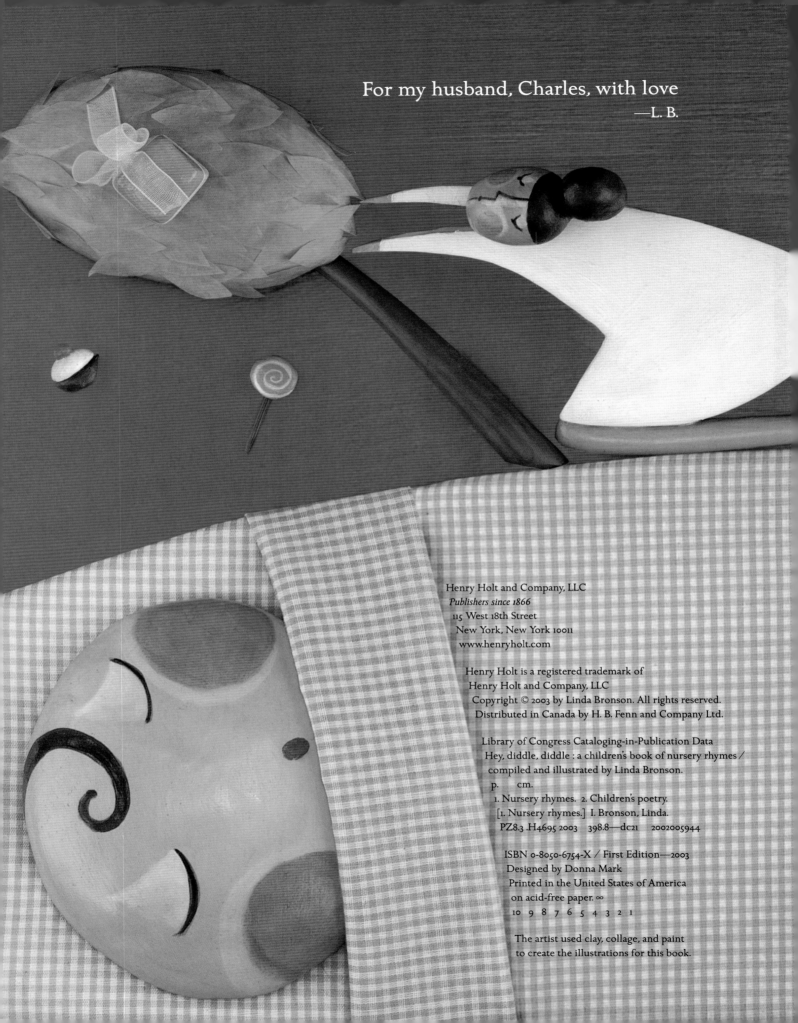

For my husband, Charles, with love
—L. B.

Henry Holt and Company, LLC
Publishers since 1866
115 West 18th Street
New York, New York 10011
www.henryholt.com

Henry Holt is a registered trademark of
Henry Holt and Company, LLC
Copyright © 2003 by Linda Bronson. All rights reserved.
Distributed in Canada by H. B. Fenn and Company Ltd.

Library of Congress Cataloging-in-Publication Data
Hey, diddle, diddle : a children's book of nursery rhymes /
compiled and illustrated by Linda Bronson.
p.   cm.
1. Nursery rhymes. 2. Children's poetry.
[1. Nursery rhymes.] I. Bronson, Linda.
PZ8.3 .H4695 2003   398.8—dc21   2002005944

ISBN 0-8050-6754-X / First Edition—2003
Designed by Donna Mark
Printed in the United States of America
on acid-free paper. ∞
10 9 8 7 6 5 4 3 2 1

The artist used clay, collage, and paint
to create the illustrations for this book.

Hey, Diddle, Diddle

A Children's Book of Nursery Rhymes

Compiled and illustrated by **Linda Bronson**

Henry Holt and Company · New York

Contents

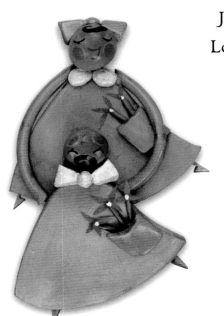

Humpty Dumpty sat on a wall,
Humpty Dumpty had a great fall.
All the king's horses, and all the king's men,
Couldn't put Humpty together again.

8

Jack and Jill went up the hill,
To fetch a pail of water.
Jack fell down and broke his crown,
And Jill came tumbling after.

London Bridge is falling down,
Falling down, falling down.
London Bridge is falling down,
My fair lady.

Hickory, dickory, dock!
The mouse ran up the clock.
The clock struck One,
The mouse ran down.
Hickory, dickory, dock!

Old Mother Hubbard
Went to her cupboard,
To give her poor dog a bone.
But when she got there,
The cupboard was bare,
And so the poor dog had none.

One, two, three, four,
Mary at the cottage door.
Five, six, seven, eight,
Eating cherries off a plate.

Pease porridge hot,
Pease porridge cold,
Pease porridge in the pot,
Nine days old.
Some like it hot,
Some like it cold,
Some like it in the pot,
Nine days old.

Little Miss Muffet
Sat on a tuffet,
Eating her curds and whey.
Along came a spider,
Who sat down beside her,
And frightened Miss Muffet away.

Hey, diddle, diddle,
The cat and the fiddle,
The cow jumped over the moon.
The little dog laughed
To see such sport,
And the dish ran away with the spoon.

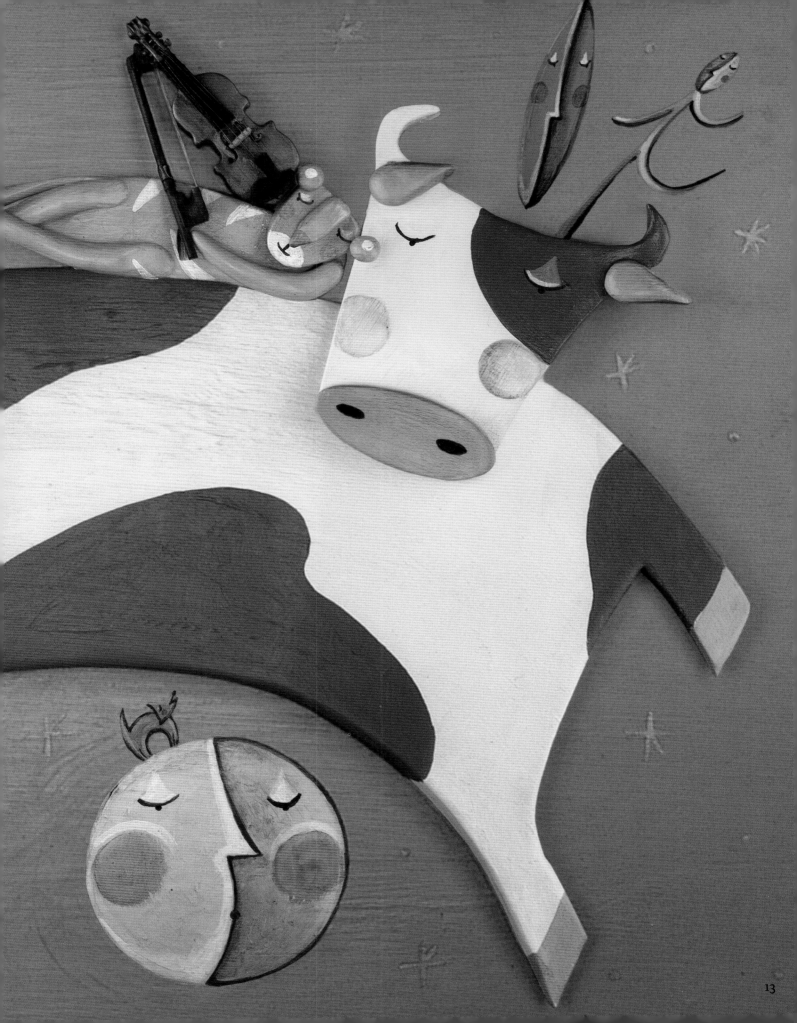

Rain, rain, go away,
Come again another day.
Little Johnny wants to play.

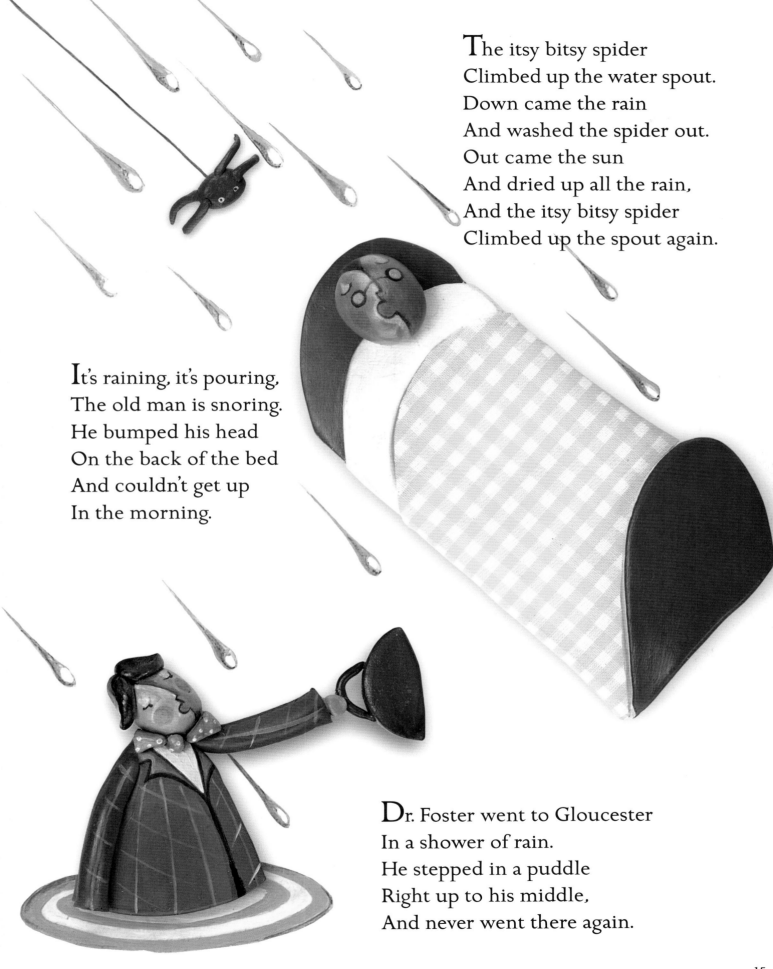

The itsy bitsy spider
Climbed up the water spout.
Down came the rain
And washed the spider out.
Out came the sun
And dried up all the rain,
And the itsy bitsy spider
Climbed up the spout again.

It's raining, it's pouring,
The old man is snoring.
He bumped his head
On the back of the bed
And couldn't get up
In the morning.

Dr. Foster went to Gloucester
In a shower of rain.
He stepped in a puddle
Right up to his middle,
And never went there again.

Little Boy Blue,
  come blow your horn.
The sheep's in the meadow,
  the cow's in the corn.

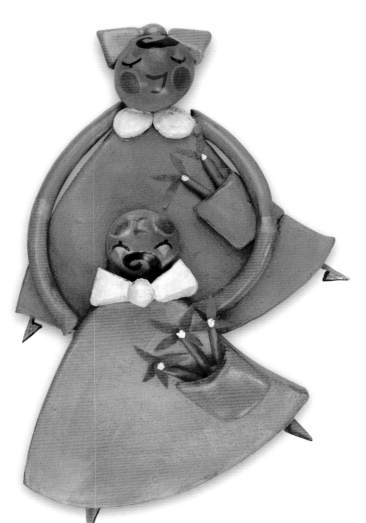

Ring around the rosies,
A pocket full of posies.
Ashes! Ashes!
We all fall down!

Peter Piper picked a peck
  of pickled peppers.
A peck of pickled peppers
  Peter Piper picked.
If Peter Piper picked a peck
  of pickled peppers,
How many peppers
  did Peter Piper pick?

Mary, Mary, quite contrary,
How does your garden grow?
With silver bells and cockle shells,
And pretty maids all in a row.

Little Robin Redbreast,
   sat upon a tree.
Up went Pussycat,
   down went he.
Down came Pussycat,
   away Robin ran.
Says little Robin Redbreast,
   "Catch me if you can!"

Of all the gay birds that I ever did see,
The owl is the fairest by far to me.
For all the day long she sits on a tree,
And when the night comes, away flies she.

Mary had a pretty bird,
Feathers bright and yellow.
Slender legs, upon my word,
He was a pretty fellow.
The sweetest notes he always sung,
Which much delighted Mary,
And near the cage she'd always sit,
To hear her own canary.

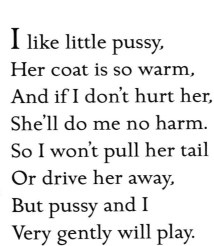

I like little pussy,
Her coat is so warm,
And if I don't hurt her,
She'll do me no harm.
So I won't pull her tail
Or drive her away,
But pussy and I
Very gently will play.

Here we go round the mulberry bush,
The mulberry bush, the mulberry bush.
Here we go round the mulberry bush,
On a cold and frosty morning.

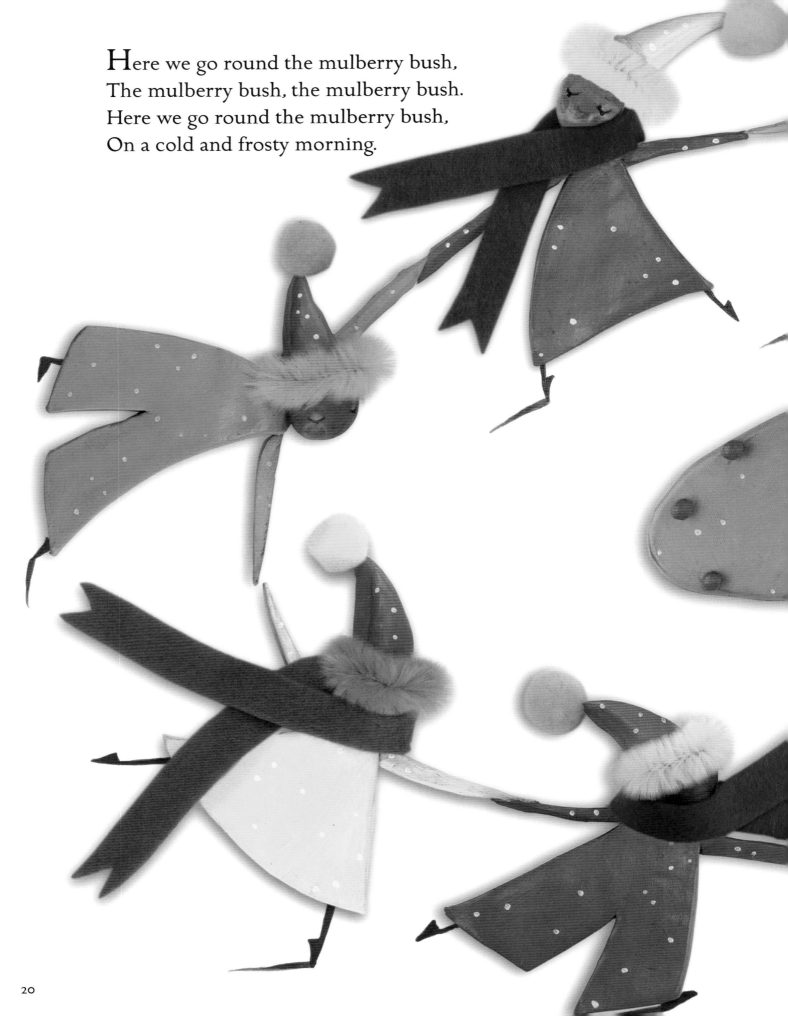

Mary had a little lamb,
Its fleece was white as snow,
And everywhere that Mary went
The lamb was sure to go.

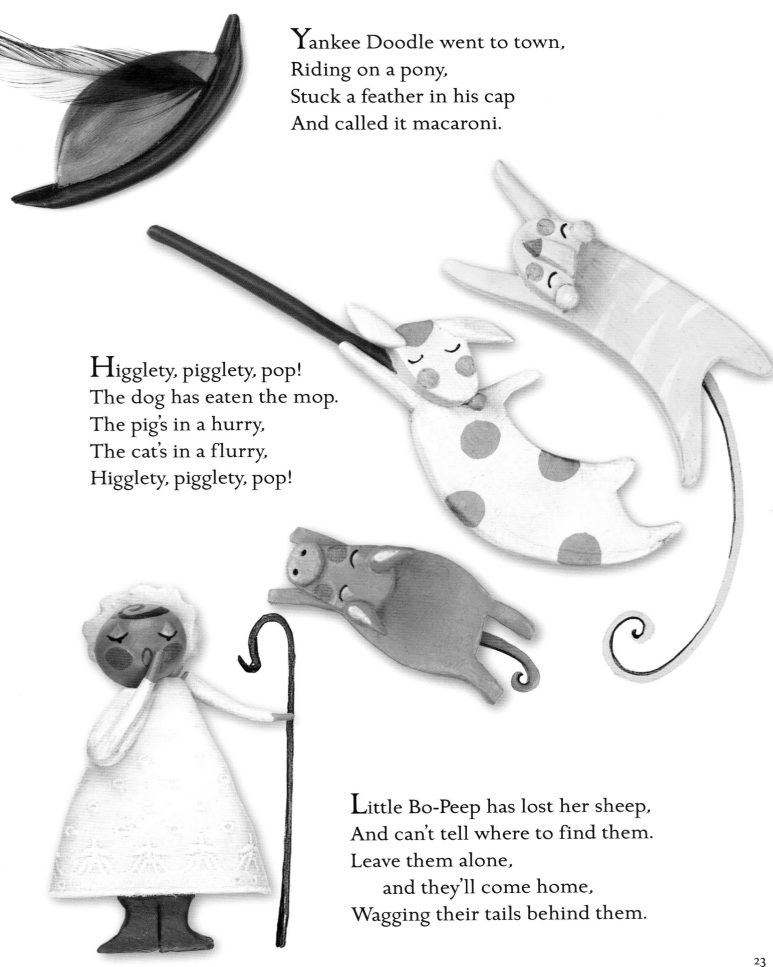

Yankee Doodle went to town,
Riding on a pony,
Stuck a feather in his cap
And called it macaroni.

Higglety, pigglety, pop!
The dog has eaten the mop.
The pig's in a hurry,
The cat's in a flurry,
Higglety, pigglety, pop!

Little Bo-Peep has lost her sheep,
And can't tell where to find them.
Leave them alone,
    and they'll come home,
Wagging their tails behind them.

Little Tommy Tittlemouse
Lived in a little house.
He caught fishes
In other men's ditches.

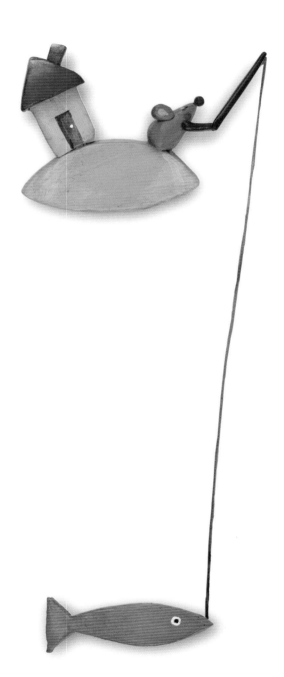

Dance to your daddy,
My little baby.
Dance to your daddy,
My little lamb.
You shall have a fishy,
In a little dishy,
You shall have a fishy,
When the boat comes in.

Swan swam over the sea.
Swim, swan, swim.
Swan swam back again.
Well swum, swan!

I had a little nut tree, nothing would it bear,
But a silver nutmeg and a golden pear.
The king of Spain's daughter came to visit me,
And all was because of my little nut tree.

Peter, Peter, pumpkin-eater,
Had a wife and couldn't keep her.
He put her in a pumpkin shell,
And there he kept her very well.

Baa, baa, black sheep,
Have you any wool?
Yes sir, yes sir,
Three bags full.

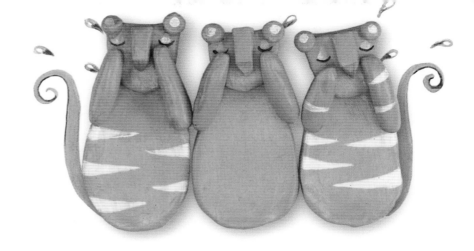

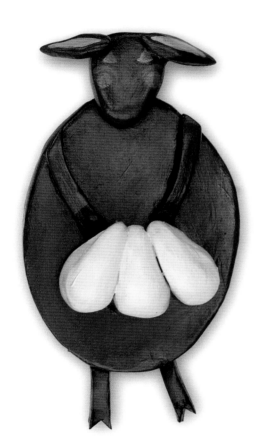

Three little kittens
Lost their mittens,
And they began to cry:
"Oh, mother dear, we sadly fear
That we have lost our mittens."
"Oh dear, don't fear,
My little kittens,
Come in and have some pie."

To market, to market, to buy a fat pig,
Home again, home again, jiggety jig.
To market, to market, to buy a fat hog,
Home again, home again, jiggety jog.

Pat a cake, pat a cake, baker's man!
Bake me a cake as fast as you can.
Pat it, and prick it, and mark it with a B,
And put it in the oven for baby and me.

Old King Cole
Was a merry old soul,
And a merry old soul was he.
He called for his pipe,
And he called for his bowl,
And he called for his fiddlers three.

"Pussycat, Pussycat,
Where have you been?"
"I've been to London
To visit the Queen."
"Pussycat, Pussycat,
What did you there?"
"I frightened a little mouse
Under my chair."

Curly Locks! Curly Locks!
Will you be mine?
You won't have to wash dishes,
Or feed the swine,
But sit on a cushion,
And sew a fine seam,
And feed upon strawberries,
Sugar, and cream.

Sing a song of sixpence,
A pocket full of rye,
Four-and-twenty blackbirds,
Baked in a pie!
When the pie was opened,
The birds began to sing.
Wasn't that a dainty dish
To set before the king?

She sells
Seashells,
By the seashore.

If all the world were apple pie,
And all the sea were ink,
And all the trees were bread and cheese,
What would we have to drink?

Bobby Shaftoe's gone to sea,
Silver buckles on his knee,
He'll come back and marry me,
Pretty Bobby Shaftoe!

Rub-a-dub-dub,
Three men in a tub,
And who do you think they'd be?
The Butcher, the Baker,
The Candlestick-maker,
Turn 'em out, knaves all three.

Jack Sprat could eat no fat,
His wife could eat no lean.
And so between them both, you see,
They licked the platter clean.

Little Jack Horner
Sat in the corner,
Eating his Christmas pie.
He put in his thumb
And pulled out a plum
And said, "What a good boy am I!"

Polly, put the kettle on,
Polly, put the kettle on,
Polly, put the kettle on,
We'll all have tea.
Sukey, take it off again,
Sukey, take it off again,
Sukey, take it off again,
They've all gone away.

Hot cross buns!
Hot cross buns!
One a penny, two a penny,
Hot cross buns!

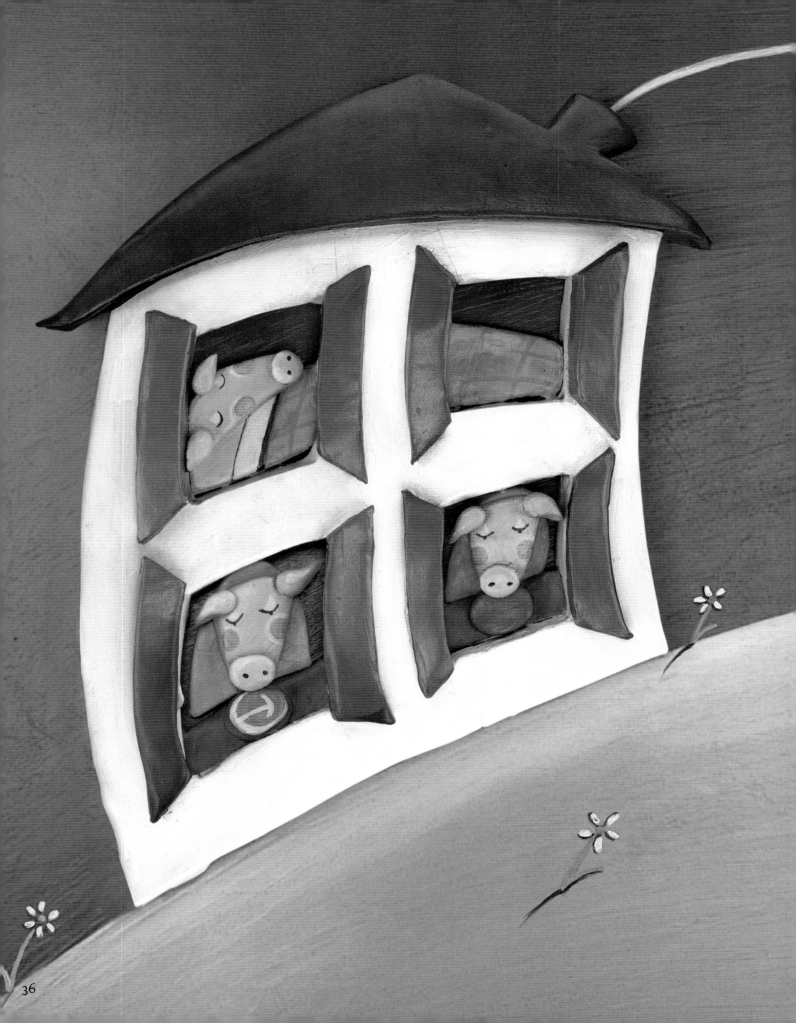

This little piggy went to market.
This little piggy stayed home.
This little piggy had roast beef.
This little piggy had none.
This little piggy cried
"Wee wee wee wee"
All the way home.

There was an old woman
who lived in a shoe.
She had so many children,
she didn't know what to do.
She gave them some broth
without any bread.
She kissed them all sweetly
and sent them to bed.

One, two, buckle my shoe.
Three, four, knock on the door.
Five, six, pick up sticks.
Seven, eight, lay them straight.

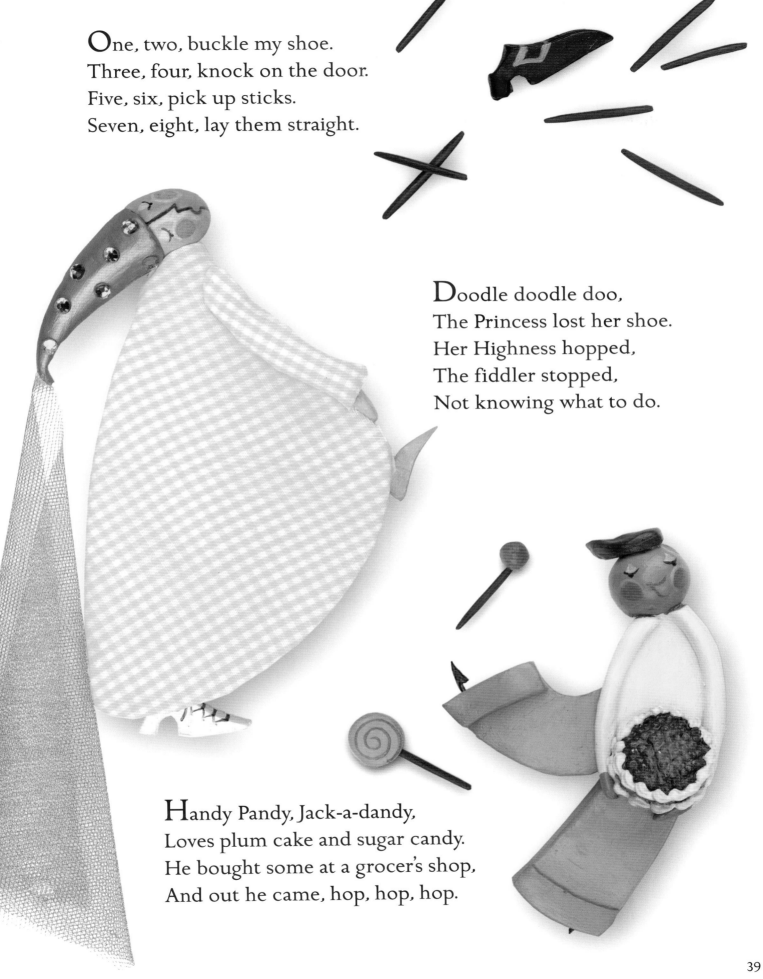

Doodle doodle doo,
The Princess lost her shoe.
Her Highness hopped,
The fiddler stopped,
Not knowing what to do.

Handy Pandy, Jack-a-dandy,
Loves plum cake and sugar candy.
He bought some at a grocer's shop,
And out he came, hop, hop, hop.

Fiddle dee dee, fiddle dee dee,
The Fly married the Bumblebee.
Parson Beetle married the Pear,
And they all went out to take the air.

Old Mother Goose,
When she wanted to wander,
Would ride through the air
On a very fine gander.

And Old Mother Goose,
The goose saddled soon,
And mounting its back,
Flew up to the moon.

Hickety, pickety, my black hen,
She lays eggs for gentlemen.
Sometimes nine,
Sometimes ten.
Hickety, pickety, my black hen.

Hush-a-bye, baby, on the tree top,
When the wind blows, the cradle will rock.
When the bough bends the cradle will fall,
And down will come baby, cradle, and all.

Come to the window,
My baby, with me,
And look at the stars
That shine on the sea!
There are two little stars
That play at bo-peep
With two little fish
Far down in the deep,
And two little frogs
Cry "Neap, neap, neap."
I see a dear baby
That should be asleep.

Diddle, diddle, dumpling, my son John,
Went to bed with his stockings on,
One shoe off, and one shoe on,
Diddle, diddle, dumpling, my son John.

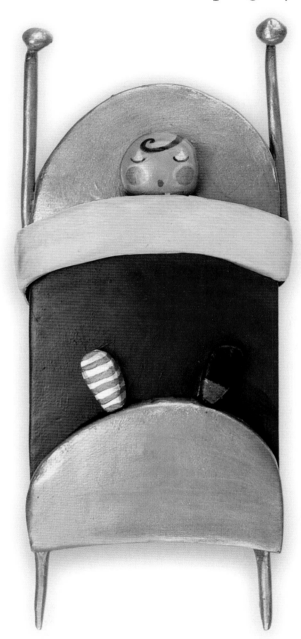

Wee Willie Winkie
    runs through the town,
Upstairs and downstairs
    in his nightgown,
Rapping at the window,
    crying through the lock,
"Are the children in their beds?
    For now it's ten o'clock!"

Twinkle, twinkle, little star,
How I wonder what you are!
Up above the world so high,
Like a diamond in the sky.
Twinkle, twinkle, little star,
How I wonder what you are!

Sleep, baby, sleep,
Thy father guards the sheep.
Thy mother shakes
The dreamland tree,
And from it fall
Sweet dreams for thee,
Sleep, baby, sleep.

44